The Littlest DINOSAUR

MICHAEL FOREMAN

BLOOMSBURY

LONDON OXFORD NEW YORK NEW DELHI SYDNEY

Long, long ago when the world was young
and everything was new, a mother dinosaur sat proudly
amongst her eggs.

The Littlest DINOSAUR

To Chloe
with love

Bloomsbury Publishing, London, Oxford, New York, New Delhi and Sydney

First published in Great Britain in 2008 by Bloomsbury Publishing Plc
50 Bedford Square, London, WC1B 3DP

A CIP catalogue record of this book is available from the British Library

ISBN 978 0 7475 8984 6 (HB)
ISBN 978 0 7475 8985 3 (PB)

Printed in Italy

3 5 7 9 8 6 4 2

All papers used by Bloomsbury Publishing are natural, recyclable products made
from wood grown in well-managed forests. The manufacturing processes conform
to the environmental regulations of the country of origin.

One by one, the eggs began to crack, and baby dinosaurs poked their heads out into the sunshine. All except one.

The mother worried and fussed about it, and kept it warm and sang songs to it. But still the egg didn't crack.

The neighbours came with help and advice.
"Make it warmer," they said.
"Keep it cool," they suggested.

The mother was very loving and lay beside the egg all the time. She breathed on it to keep it warm or fanned it with banana leaves to cool it down. But still the egg didn't crack.

The father dinosaur wanted to break the egg open, but the mother said, "No. It will happen when the baby is ready, not before."

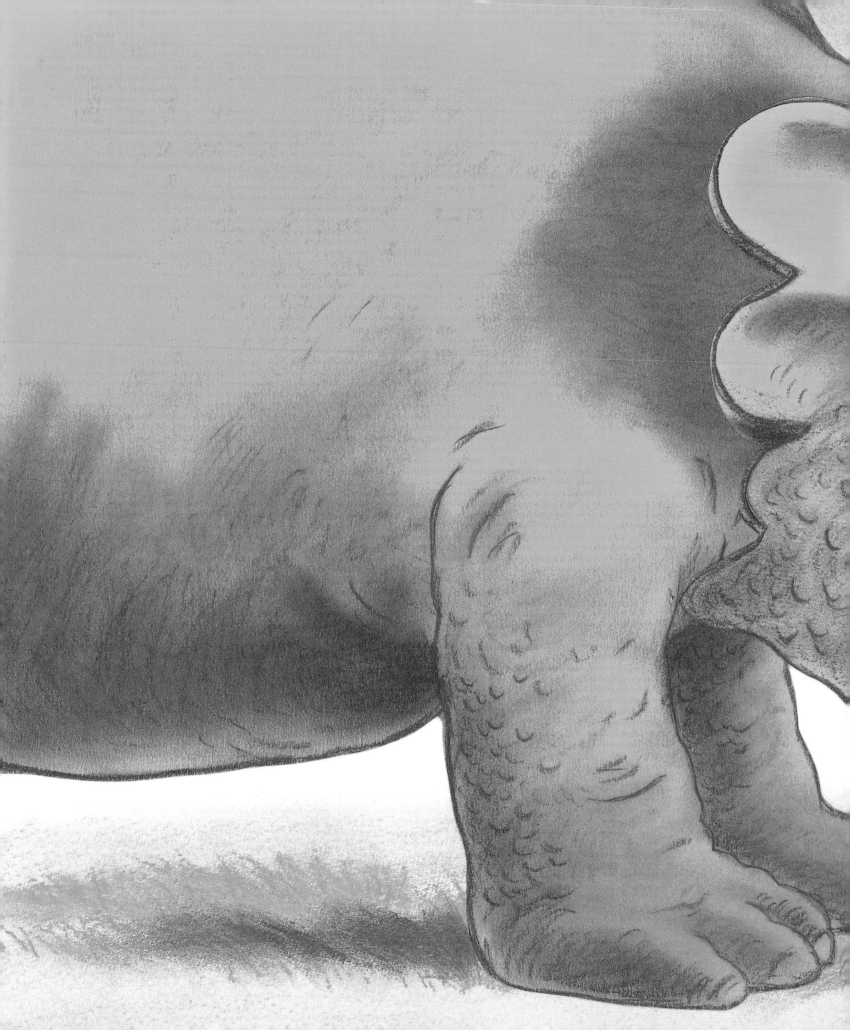

Then, one day, the father became so tired of looking after all the other young dinosaurs while the mother fussed over the egg, that he put his face very close to the egg and shouted.

"Come on, egg! **Do something!"**
The egg shook. The egg wobbled, and then began to crack.

A little crack at first, then a big crack, and the shell broke in two.

The baby dinosaur blinked in the sunlight. The father dinosaur gasped. Mother dinosaur gasped. All the young dinosaurs and all the neighbours gasped. They had never seen such a tiny baby. "That's the littlest dinosaur I have ever seen," said the father. "You're no bigger than a dinosaur's toe!"

The neighbours began to giggle.

"Oh! He may be tiny, but he's very special to me," cried Mother dinosaur and scooped the baby up and kissed his tiny face.

Days and weeks passed, and no matter how much food Mother gave the baby dinosaur, he didn't grow any bigger.

The littlest dinosaur was sad because
he was too small to join in with his
big brothers and sisters when they
played. And then there was the
worry about being trodden on
by his huge neighbours.

The only place that the littlest dinosaur felt safe was high on a hill. There he could sit and look down on the forest. It made him feel bigger. One day, far away on another hill, he saw another dinosaur.

It was a Long Neck. Even at that distance, he looked sad. The littlest dinosaur wondered how a dinosaur that big could possibly be sad.

When the rainy season began, the big dinosaurs squelched and rolled in the mud. But not the littlest dinosaur. He hated the mud. He was always getting stuck in the other dinosaurs' big muddy footprints and having to yell,
"Help! Get me out of here!"

Then, one day, the father dinosaur got stuck. He was squelching and rolling in the deep mud at the edge of the river. But when he tried to get out, he couldn't. The more he struggled, the more he got stuck.

"Get me out of here!" he yelled.

Mother tried to help, but **she** got stuck. The neighbours tried to help, and **they** got stuck. The littlest dinosaur's brothers and sisters waded in and **they** got stuck too.

"Get us out of here!" they all yelled.

The littlest dinosaur wished and wished that he was bigger. Big enough to rescue them.

"You must go for help," cried the mother dinosaur.
But who could help? wondered the littlest dinosaur.
Then he remembered the Long Neck.

The littlest dinosaur was scared as he stepped from the riverbank on to a water lily leaf. It tipped and dipped, but didn't sink.

One leaf at a time, he wibbled and wobbled his way across the
river, then ran through the forest and climbed the hill, slipping
and sliding, sliding and slipping, until he got to the top.

There he was, the Long Neck.
He looked down at the
littlest dinosaur.

"Help me, please," the littlest
dinosaur cried. "My family are
stuck in the river and the water
is rising fast!"

The Long Neck picked him up and, with great long strides, was soon down the hill, through the forest and at the riverbank. He stretched his neck across the river and began pushing and pulling the sinking dinosaurs out, until one by one they were all safe on the shore.

"Thank you!" Father dinosaur shouted as he waved to the Long Neck. "And as for you," he said, picking up the littlest dinosaur, "you may be the size of a bug, but you have the brave heart of a dinosaur one hundred times your size."
And he kissed him on his tiny nose.

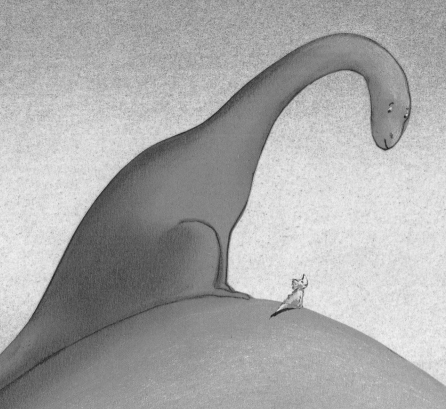

When the rains stopped
and the river was not so wide,
the littlest dinosaur went to visit the
Long Neck again. He no longer looked so sad.
"I thought I was too big and clumsy to do anything
useful," he said, "but now I know that's not true."
"And I thought I was too small to do anything at all,"
laughed the littlest dinosaur.
They sat together on the hill, the biggest and the littlest,
and now, the greatest of friends.